D0605374

The
Animals
Watched

AN ALPHABET BOOK

by John Warren Stewig

illustrated by Rosanne Litzinger

Holiday House / New York

With thanks to All Saints Episcopal Cathedral,
and Fr. Julian V. Hills   J. W. S.

For Barbara Ann   R. L.

Text copyright © 2007 by John Warren Stewig
Illustrations copyright © 2007 by Rosanne Litzinger
All Rights Reserved
Printed and Bound in Malaysia
The text typeface is Goudy Oldstyle.
The artwork was created with pencil, watercolour, gouache,
and color pencil on 140 lb. cold press fine watercolour paper.
www.holidayhouse.com
First Edition
1 3 5 7 9 10 8 6 4 2

Library of Congress Cataloging-in-Publication Data
Stewig, John W.
The animals watched / by John Warren Stewig ; illustrated by Rosanne Litzinger.— 1st ed.
p. cm.
ISBN-13: 978-0-8234-1906-7 (hardcover)
ISBN-10: 0-8234-1906-1 (hardcover)
1. Noah's ark—Juvenile literature. I. Litzinger, Rosanne. II. Title.
BS658.S75 2007
222'.1109505—dc22
2006004784

"We," said the **aardvarks**, "we saw Noah listen to the word of God, foretelling a flood because the people had been evil."

"We," said the **badgers**, "we saw Noah's family receive God's instruction to gather two of each of us onto an ark because every other living thing would perish in the flood."

"We," said the **capybaras**, "we saw Noah and his sons— Shem, Ham, and Japheth—gather the gopher wood to build an ark that would save us."

"We," said the **dingoes**, "we saw them build the ship's cedar ribs and cover them with reeds, so the ribs stretched skyward like a huge skeleton."

"We," said the **egrets**, "we saw Noah and his sons coat the inside and the outside of the ark with pitch."

"We," said the **fawns**, "we saw Noah's sons, his wife, and his sons' wives gather every kind of food to sustain us during the forty days and forty nights that God foretold the rain would fall."

"We," said the **giraffes**, "we saw Noah's sons shepherd us—
fowl, cattle, and every creeping thing—two by two up
the gangplank into the ark's hold."

"We," said the **hedgehogs**, "we saw each pair
find a place for itself, secure belowdecks."
"We," said the **iguanas**, "we saw the Lord
close the door of the ark."

"We," said the **jaguars**, "we saw that after seven days the windows of heaven opened and the deluge descended."

"We," said the **kiwis**, "we saw that everything died that had the breath of life in its nostrils."

"We," said the **lorises**, "we saw the ark float on top of the murky waters that covered the highest hills."

"We," said the **musk oxen**, "we saw the water rise fifty more cubits upward and cover the mountains."

"We," said the great crested **newts**, "we saw Noah's wife and his sons' wives bring us food to sustain us on the journey."

"We," said the **octopuses**, "we saw the rain come down for forty days."

"We," said the **penguins**, "we counted the months, as ten passed slowly by, before we could see the tops of the mountains again."

"We," said the **quetzals**, "we saw the wind pass over the earth and the waters begin to subside."

"We," said the **rheas**, "we saw the rain stop, the clouds part, and the sun's rays warm the waters."

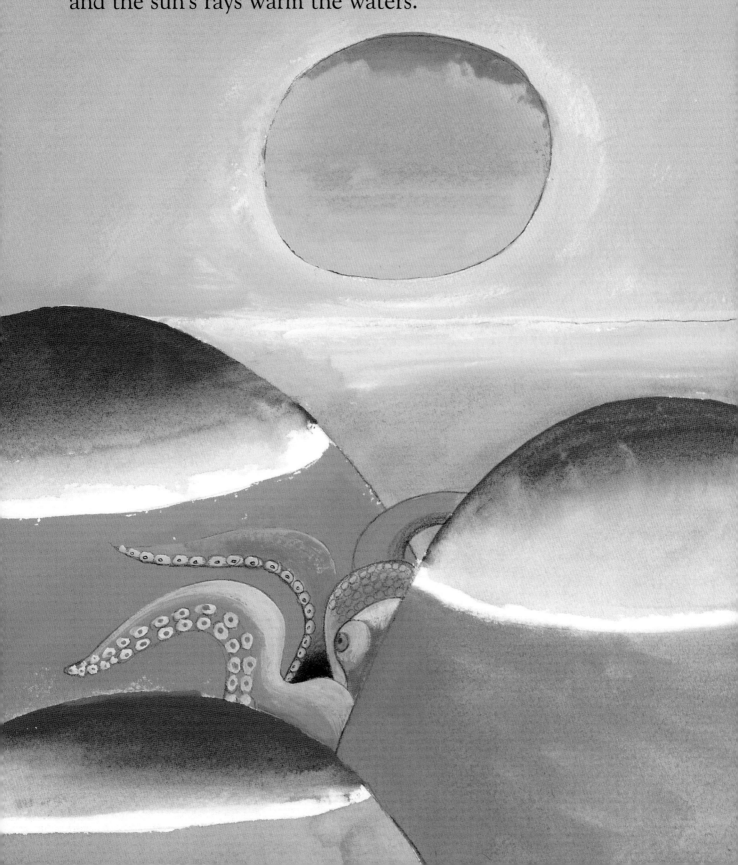

"We," said the **sheep**, "we saw Noah send forth a raven, searching for land, but we also saw it return without a sign."

"We," said the **tapirs**, "we saw Noah send forth a dove, and we saw that this time she returned bringing an olive twig."

"We," said the **urodeles**, "we saw another seven days pass, and Noah sent the dove out again; and this time she did not return."

"We," said the **vervets**, "we felt the bump as the ark came to rest on top of the mountain."

"We," said the **warthogs**, "we saw the gangplank lower so we could walk down to dry land."

"We," said the **Xoloitzcuintlis**, "we saw Noah, as each pair left to seek a place, building an altar to God."

"We," said the **yaks**, "we saw the rainbow God set in the sky and heard him say, 'I will never again send a flood to destroy my beautiful world.'"

"We," said the **zebras**, "we saw the sons and daughters of Noah follow God's instruction to go forth and multiply, filling the whole earth."

Animal Alphabet Glossary

 The **aardvark** burrows underground in African savannas. It is nocturnal, which means that it's awake at night. Its 18-inch tongue can trap food in its sticky saliva.

 The sturdy **badger** is a nocturnal mammal that lives in a burrow (or sett). It eats small rodents.

 The **capybara** (kap-uh-BEAR-uh) is a South American rodent. It can grow up to 4 feet in length, not counting its tail because it doesn't have one.

 The **dingo** is a wild dog descended from domesticated Asian dogs. It is usually ginger colored and lives in Australia.

 The **egret**, a wading bird, uses its daggerlike bill to spear food. It grows long plumes (or showy feathers) in breeding season.

 The **fawn** is a young deer that still drinks its mother's milk. It may grow up to live as long as forty years.

 The 15-to-18-feet-tall **giraffe** is the tallest of all four-legged animals. Giraffes live on savannas in Africa.

 The **hedgehog** is covered with both hair and spines. It sleeps during the day after dining on insects and hibernates in winter.

 The dark-colored **iguana** seeks the sun because it cannot regulate its own body temperature. It eats plants and is itself eaten by humans.

 The **jaguar**, which lives in Central and South America, is bigger than its cousin the leopard. It uses its acute sense of smell to find prey.

 The **kiwi** is covered in loose and fluffy feathers like those of a young bird. It can't fly because its wings are very small compared with its body size, but it gets around well on its stout legs.

 The **loris** lives in trees in Southeast Asia, Sri Lanka, and India. It uses its extremely strong fingers and toes to move quickly from branch to branch.

 The heavyset **musk ox** needs a thick coat because it lives only in Greenland and near the Arctic Circle in North America.

 The **newt** is a tiny, semiaquatic salamander that looks like a scaleless lizard. It breathes through gills when it's young.

 The **octopus** has eight arms, or tentacles, surrounding its head. Each arm has two rows of suckers that help it move through the water.

 The **penguin** is a web-footed flightless bird that walks upright on its short legs. It lives in the Southern Hemisphere from Antarctica to near the equator.

 The **quetzal** (keht-SAHL), whose Spanish name means "brilliant tail feathers," lives in Central America.

 The **rhea** (REE-ah) is a tall South American bird that has three toes on each foot.

 The **sheep** has a four-part stomach and chews food it has previously swallowed, making it a ruminant mammal. It has long been domesticated for its wool, milk, and flesh.

 The **tapir** (TAY-per), a relative of the horse, has hooves rather than feet. It sleeps during the day and is hunted for food.

 The cold-blooded **urodele** (YOUR-ah-deel) has no voice at all. It breathes air as an adult but gives birth to young that breathe through gills.

 The **vervet** monkey is primarily frugivorous, which means it is a fruit eater. It lives in southern and eastern Africa, where it is considered a pest and is often killed.

 The **warthog**, a relative of the domestic pig, has protruding tusks that can frighten away African neighbors. It wallows in the mud for protection from the sun.

 The **Xoloitzcuintlis** (show-low-eets-QUEEN-tli) is a small Mexican dog that is only 11 to 12 inches tall. It has very little hair but very large ears.

 The long-haired **yak** lives in the Himalayan Mountains in central Asia and Tibet. Yaks are both wild and domesticated and live in areas of permanent snow.

 The **zebra**, a mammal related to the horse, is native to central and southern Africa. Its stripes serve as camouflage against its main predator, the lion.